JANET S. WONG

Me and Rolly Maloo

Illustrated by

ELIZABETH BUTTLER

Charlesbridge

To Judy O'Malley—J. S. W.

For Tom & Tyler—E. B.

First paperback edition 2013
Text copyright © 2010 by Janet S. Wong
Illustrations copyright © 2010 by Elizabeth Buttler

Published by Charlesbridge, 85 Main Street, Watertown, MA 02472
(617) 926-0329 • www.charlesbridge.com

Library of Congress Cataloging-in-Publication Data
Wong, Janet S.
    Me and Rolly Maloo / Janet Wong ; illustrated by Elizabeth Buttler.
        p. cm.
    Summary: An unpopular girl cheats on a math test when the most popular girl in school asks her to give her answers.
    ISBN 978-1-58089-158-5 (reinforced for library use)
    ISBN 978-1-58089-159-2 (softcover)
[1. Cheating—Fiction. 2. Mathematics—Fiction. 3. Popularity—Fiction. 4. Schools—Fiction.] I. Buttler, Elizabeth, ill. II. Title.
PZ7.W842115Me 2010
[Fic]—dc22   2009026883

Printed in the United States of America
(hc) 10 9 8 7 6 5 4 3 2 1
(sc) 10 9 8 7 6 5 4 3 2 1

Illustrations were created in pencil and Adobe Photoshop
Display type set in Monotype Knock Out and Mister Earl;
    dialog type set in Blambot, designed by Nate Piekos;
    and text type set in Century Schoolbook
Printed June 2013 by Worzalla Publishing Company,
    Stevens Point, Wisconsin, USA
Production supervision by Brian G. Walker
Designed by Susan Mallory Sherman, Sindy Limin, and Whitney Leader-Picone

Table of Contents

Cast of Characters

Jenna Lee

Nelly Lee

(Jenna's mom)

Rolly Maloo

Kath Maloo

(Rolly's mom)

Patty Parker

Annabee Parker

(Patty's mom)

Shorn L. Loop

Diane Loop

(Shorn L.'s mom)

Dolores Pie

(the teacher)

Hugo Johns

Michelle Young

(the principal)

1 Rolly Maloo and Me

Ring, ring! Ring, ring! Ring, ring—

The third day of fourth grade, Rolly Maloo called me up at home. Out of the blue, for no reason at all, she asked me if I wanted to come to her house to play. Rolly Maloo has air conditioning, I bet. But even if her house were ten times hotter than ours, I would go in an Appaloosa minute.

Rolly Maloo is the most popular anybody (girl or boy) in fourth grade and maybe even the history of the whole school, except for her older sister. Marissa Maloo left Edison last year for fifth grade at Hilltop, the fancy private school downtown.

Rolly Maloo spends every recess in the middle

of a crowd of kids who let her say everything she wants. I spend every recess sitting under a tree, digging holes in the mud with Shorn L.

Rolly Maloo, what on earth has you calling me, Jenna P. Lee, for no plain reason at all?

No one had ever called me up special to ask if I wanted to come to their house to play. Never. Except Shorn L. did once, but that doesn't count for much around school, because I am the only one who likes Shorn L. And even though I do like Shorn L., I won't go back to her house, because nobody wants to be fooled by a bunch of Shorn L.'s brothers dropping ground-up bugs in your pop.

When I heard Rolly Maloo say her own beautiful name, I

couldn't believe my good luck. I felt so special. I felt chosen. Then I wondered if she had called the wrong number. She said my name three times in a row. I guess she thought she had the wrong number because I couldn't talk with my mouth hanging open. When I finally croaked out my hello, Rolly asked, "Jenna, you want to come over?"

O-D-D, and doesn't even know how to talk on a phone. You'd never guess she's the best at math in all of Edison Elementary — a regular Alberta Einstein (and just as strange)!

I twirled and twirled until I tied myself up in the telephone cord like a rope-tied cow at the rodeo.

While I was busy untwirling, I didn't hear what Rolly was saying. I realized later on that she was saying something about the math test, but if you asked me then, I'd say she was talking about lunch. This is because I was busy thinking of us sitting together at lunch. I would share my every-day apple and she would share her cafeteria cake. While she was chewing, everyone would listen to everything I had to say for once. Shorn L. could come sit at our table, too. Maybe not the first week, but later on, once I got the okay from Rolly.

I said, "You know, Rolly, I could bring my special spinner toy to your house, you'll really like it. And my gray Arabian horse, the one with the red leather saddle." I was so excited I said "leather," even though it's really made of plastic. As soon as I made the mistake, I started to worry that Rolly Maloo would consider me a liar. "Sheesh-O-Mighty, light the liar on fire!" is what Shorn L. would say, except she says "liar" like "lawyer," and no one would ever accuse me of being one of those.

Again Rolly said something-something about math and something, but math was the last thing on my mind. Then I heard Rolly's mother remind her to remind me to ask my mother if it was okay. I said, "I'm sure it's okay." I pressed the phone against my chest and shouted out to Momma in the laundry room. Momma shouted back that she couldn't hear me. I left Rolly hanging on, and I ran over to the laundry room to ask.

Momma did not even stop to think. She said, "No, not today." How about tomorrow, I started to ask, but she put on that four o'clock frown of hers, and she said, "Don't give me that. You know you have your chores."

9

I lied to Rolly. "Maybe tomorrow," I said. Rolly did not say "Maybe tomorrow" back. We hung up, and I knew I had missed my chance.

Every once in a while you get a chance, and it's there, and then it's gone. I felt my chosen feeling falling away. Something had gotten into Rolly Maloo for the meantime, but it might not be there ever again.

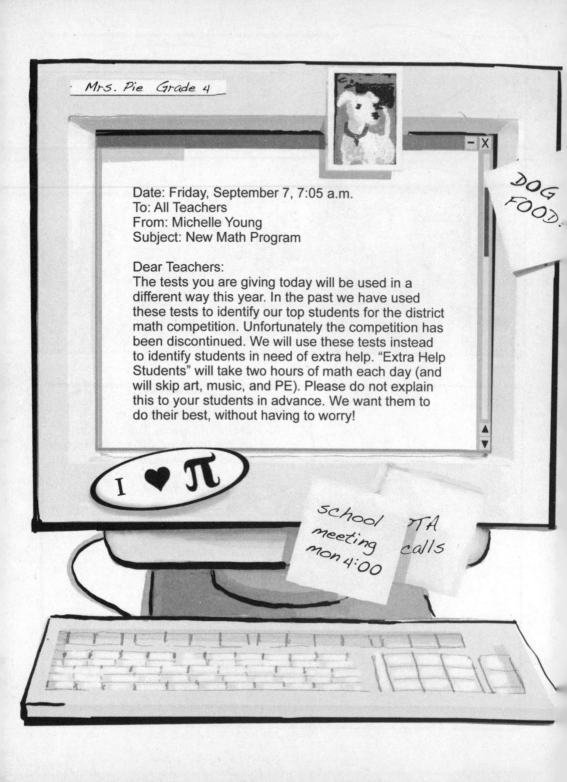

Mrs. Pie Grade 4

DOG FOOD!

Date: Friday, September 7, 7:05 a.m.
To: All Teachers
From: Michelle Young
Subject: New Math Program

Dear Teachers:
The tests you are giving today will be used in a different way this year. In the past we have used these tests to identify our top students for the district math competition. Unfortunately the competition has been discontinued. We will use these tests instead to identify students in need of extra help. "Extra Help Students" will take two hours of math each day (and will skip art, music, and PE). Please do not explain this to your students in advance. We want them to do their best, without having to worry!

I ♥ π

school meeting mon 4:00

PTA calls

2 Mrs. Pie and I

I have been waiting for four years to be a student of Mrs. Dolores Pie, who has taught fourth grade at our school ever since before I was born. It was one full week before kindergarten and my mother brought me to the school to sign up. The office lady said too late, no more space. Such a mean voice, a laughing-at-you voice. No space left for me.

Mrs. Pie followed us out. She told my mother not to worry. She drove us to the district office in her car, which smelled like gardenias. Walked into the district office holding my hand and made everyone treat us important.

Some people think teachers can't be your friends. I guess Mrs. Pie isn't our friend, exactly, but I know she cares deeply about us kids. Like an aunt. Like a grandmother. Well, like a really good teacher.

Three things that make Mrs. Pie happy:

1. Fresh gardenias
2. Brand-new books
3. Children who know alphabetical order

The first day of kindergarten, Momma baked a "thank-you pie" for Mrs. Pie because of her name and because her eyes look so round and dark and creamy, just like Momma's best chocolate cream pies. The fourth graders looked at me funny when I delivered it. But guess what? Mrs. Pie brought me a surprise slice at lunch. She sat at my picnic table, swung her legs round like she was five years old, and said, "I am so happy to know you, Jenna Lee."

Mrs. Pie is not all sweet, though. If you do something wrong, she will tighten up her lips like she just ate a bitter lemon. Once she caught me hanging upside down from a tree. Now I don't see what's so wrong about that, but she plucked me out of the sky and called Momma. At home Momma ranted on about breaking my neck and busting my skull, and believe me, that put an end to my days in the trees. So don't do anything wrong around her: that's the short and simple of it. But when you do right by Mrs. Pie, everything tastes like sweet-chocolate-cream thank you.

3 The Math Test

Friday morning I got to school late, as usual. Late again! I wish Momma could wake up earlier, but poor Momma is always so sleepy. She stays up late stuffing envelopes for pay. Too late.

Or I wish Momma would let me walk by myself. I like to wake up early. I would love to walk to school by myself. But she's afraid of bad men hiding in the bushes.

I waved at Rolly when I sat down, but I didn't catch her eye. I tried to catch her eye again during morning reading, but Rolly was busy being her good reading self and didn't look up once the whole twenty minutes. Shorn L. made a choking noise and put a pretend "I-think-I'm-gonna-die" look on her face that made me almost bust up laughing, but thankfully I got my sillies under control pretty quick. And then we had the math test.

Do well, children. I don't want any of you to give up your PE or art or music time.

Rotten test—

At the beginning of each grade we get a special math test to see how we're doing. The kids who do the best get to compete on a team at the district math contest. It's usually three fifth graders, one fourth grader, and me. This year, now that I'm a fourth grader, it might be four fifth graders and me—or maybe somebody new. I hope somebody new gets to go.

It's not a hard contest, just a couple dozen questions, usually word problems with lots of fractions and decimals and percents. I love percents. Every time I go shopping with Momma, we work on percents. Like: What's a shirt cost when it starts out at $9.99, then gets knocked off 50 percent and you can take an extra 20 percent off at the register? A darn good deal is what most people would say, but I like to figure out the exact amount.

At the district competition I often come up with the right answer, but no one ever believes me. Our team gives the wrong answer, and when the other team gives my right answer, my teammates look at me and shrug "sorry." Our school never wins. I don't mind, though, because the main part is an all-you-can-eat lunch.

Momma loves the district math contest lunch. It is the best gift I can give her (and free at that). Momma is smaller than me sideways, but she can eat more than a circus strongman, and we go back for thirds and fourths at the lunch buffet. Those district ladies really fancy it up, with toothpicks in the sandwiches, potato salad, macaroni, Jell-O, fruit, sour greens, three kinds of ice cream, chopped nuts, whipped cream by the bucket, chocolate sauce, and cherries.

In most subjects I'm just so-so, but in math I am the best. And that is no bragging, but the red-hot truth. Last year I got 100 percent twenty times. Momma never looks at my grades, so the best part about getting 100 percent was I got glow-in-the-dark stars as rewards. I climbed onto my chair and stuck all twenty stars on the ceiling of my closet.

Somotimes I put my sleeping bag in there and slide the doors shut. When I squeeze down inside the bag, it makes me feel like I'm camping by the river.

Six things that make me happy:

1. Making my paper horses
2. Getting 100 percent on my math tests
3. Chocolate
4. Camping by the river
5. Playing basketball in PE
6. Watching Momma eat a fourth plate at the lunch buffet

Five minutes after we got the test, I was halfway through. Then I got stumped. Number eight was really hard. But the harder a problem is, the more I love it. "This is fifth-grade math," Mrs. Pie had said when she passed the tests down each row. "So don't worry if you don't get all

the answers. Remember what I said about skipping the hard questions and coming back later. Double-check your answers on the easy questions. A right answer is a right answer, if the question is easy or hard."

I like it when the questions are hard. Just like Mrs. Pie says, math is kind of like basketball: the challenge makes it fun. The game wouldn't be half as exciting if the hoop were put at five feet tall!

I got deep inside question number eight like I was squeezing deepest down into my sleeping bag in the nightglow closet. The AC was blowing so hard and cold it actually was starting to feel like camp at midnight. And all of a sudden I could see another star in the closet sky. Fuzzy at first, then shining bright.

The answer had come.

Right after I got the answer, a small paper ball hit me straight in my right ear. It was a note from Rolly Maloo. "What's #8?" it said.

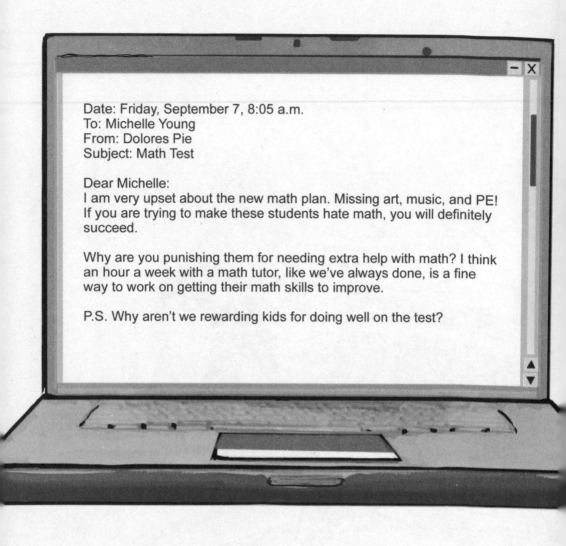

Date: Friday, September 7, 8:05 a.m.
To: Michelle Young
From: Dolores Pie
Subject: Math Test

Dear Michelle:
I am very upset about the new math plan. Missing art, music, and PE!
If you are trying to make these students hate math, you will definitely
succeed.

Why are you punishing them for needing extra help with math? I think
an hour a week with a math tutor, like we've always done, is a fine
way to work on getting their math skills to improve.

P.S. Why aren't we rewarding kids for doing well on the test?

Mrs. Pie Grade 4

DOG FOOD!!

Date: Friday, September 7, 8:55 a.m.
To: Dolores Pie
From: Michelle Young
Subject: Re: Math Test

Dear Dolores:
I understand that you are upset by our new math plan. It upsets me, too, but this is the new school district plan, not mine. And though some children will be unhappy about missing art, music, and PE, we both know that our district's math test scores must improve; we have too many students who are not passing their standardized tests. Sorry, Dolores, but there is nothing I can do. Let's just hope that all your students pass the test.

I ♥ π

school meeting mon 4:00

PTA calls

4 Cheating—or Not?

I looked at Mrs. Pie. She was busy reading her emails. I looked at Rolly, two seats to the right of me. She was making a pained face. Her fingers were spread out funny.

I looked at Hugo, behind us. Hugo was face-down on his desk, with his hands over his eyes like he couldn't bear to look at the test anymore. Hugo is always sick and still has to come to school, poor Hugo.

I looked at the scrap of paper again. I looked at Rolly Maloo. When I looked at her out of my right eyeball, she looked like Hugo: sick. Poor Rolly.

When somebody needs help, like food or clothes or money for the hospital, you don't call it cheating when you help them. You call it good work. Volunteering. Charity. Maybe helping Rolly Maloo with a math answer could be called charity. And instead of calling her a cheater, maybe you could call her someone who is smart enough to ask for help. And not too proud. I've heard people whispering

about how Momma is too proud to ask for help, and if she would just be smarter and not so stubborn, life could be a lot easier for us.

I doubt I could ever help Rolly Maloo in any other way. I bet she knew she might need help yesterday, and she wanted to talk it over. To explain herself. And she would've, if Momma had let me go to her house. How could I turn my back on her now?

The answer to number eight was 75 percent. Was it really going to hurt anyone if I gave this answer to Rolly? I guess it might knock somebody out of going to the district math competition. Most likely one of the fifth graders. One of the fifth graders who'd already been to the competition before and didn't listen to me at all, always pushing for his own wrong answers, even though we were supposed to work as a team. Besides, even if a fifth grader did get knocked out, Rolly deserved to go. She'd always just barely missed going, never went once. Her sister Marissa went twice.

I wrote the answer down on the paper. I looked at Mrs. Pie again. I looked around the room. No one was looking. Everyone was concentrating hard on their test, except for Shorn L., who was staring at the clock, and Hugo, whose eyes seemed to be glued to the ceiling.

As I rolled the answer up into a little ball, I almost wished that Mrs. Pie would look up at me and stop me from having to throw the answer to Rolly. Rolly made her hurting face again.

I threw the ball.

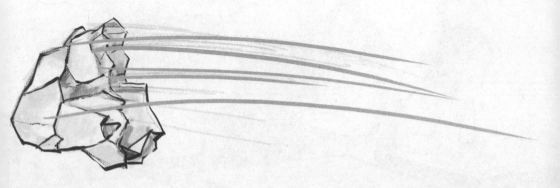

Rolly Maloo caught it, looked at the answer, and passed the ball to Patty. Then she wrote "#9" on another scrap of paper, and tossed that new piece of paper, rolled up, at me. This time, though, she threw the ball too high, and I had to stand up to catch it.

I sat down and looked up just in time to see Mrs. Pie stand up, her eyes as big as pies themselves, chocolate cream "no-thank-you" pies ready to hit me in the face.

I could feel the whole room stop breathing. No breathing, no pencil scratching, no bubbling in answers—just everyone thinking crud, crud, *crud!* Then Mrs. Pie sat back down and stared at her desk. I knew that she thought I was the one who had asked for the answer. Poor Jenna, a cheater. I wanted Mrs. Pie to stomp back and grab me and Rolly Maloo by our collars and shake out the truth, but she just stared at her desk.

What is going on?!

For five whole seconds that seemed like five whole years, Mrs. Pie stared at her desk. Then she looked at me again and walked over. "Give me the ball," she whispered. I handed her the little piece of paper soaked with my sweat.

"Stay in for recess and we'll talk. Now finish your test." As she walked back to her desk, Rolly tossed a paper ball in Patty's lap. Mrs. Pie didn't see it. She was busy reading her emails again. Or maybe Rolly didn't toss anything. I don't know. My eyes started going crazy just about then and I couldn't keep my mind still. For ten more minutes my pencil made marks on the paper, but the answers might as well have been cat scratches.

When it was time to get in line for recess, Rolly Maloo rushed to the front of the line. I tried to catch her eye from my seat, but she wouldn't look at me.

5 Confession Time

"Who threw the ball to you, Jenna?" Mrs. Pie asked. I wanted to say Rolly, but I could not say her name. What if Rolly did want to have me come to her house ever again? She wouldn't if I told on her. I felt prickles in my throat. "Someone threw you the paper ball," she said. "You need to tell."

"No one," I said, and kept my eyes looking down at my shoes.

I have never been any good at doing anything wrong. Other people can cheat and lie and never get caught. Me, I do a just slightly bad thing and get busted to bits and pieces. Except Mrs. Pie didn't bust me. Worse than that, she patted my shoulder. "You have a real talent for math, Jenna," she said. "You could be my best math student ever."

Could have been, I thought. I could have been.

"You still can be," Mrs. Pie said. Did I accidentally say my thoughts out loud? If Mrs. Pie could read my mind about that, could she also read my mind about Rolly?

Rolly, Rolly, Rolly, I thought, trying to send the message to Mrs. Pie's brain without actually saying anything. Mrs. Pie, Rolly did it. But please don't punish us. I'm sure she didn't mean it, and I will be an angel for the rest of the year—I swear!

"Please don't tell my momma," I said, and wished I hadn't said it as soon as it came out my mouth. Now I knew she would tell her for sure.

"Recess is almost over," Mrs. Pie said. She opened her desk drawer and took out a packet of pretzels. "Why don't you just sit back down and have a little snack. Let's keep this quiet, between us."

6 Rumors

Mrs. Pie did not tell my momma. From what I can see, she did not tell anybody. Shorn L. quizzed me at lunch and I told her exactly what happened, but she already knew more than I did. (I guess she wasn't looking at the clock the whole time.) Shorn L. thought for sure she'd be asked to stay after school, being, as she put it, "The Number One Suspicious Friend-in-Need." But nope, no questions asked, no funny looks from Mrs. Pie, nothing. I was dying to talk to Rolly, but she still wouldn't look my way. Shorn L. gave her a new nickname, "User," that she hissed at her when she walked by, but Rolly didn't even blink. Patty hissed back, "Loser!" while still managing a smile on her face. I've got to admit that Patty is pretty swift. Ouch. Shorn L. said "User" again, but it sounded kind of flat.

I believe Mrs. Pie didn't say a single thing about the paper ball to anyone. Just like they do in the movies, I pinched myself to make sure this wasn't just a bad dream.

Momma was waiting for me after school at the mailbox, where she can look three blocks up the street to the school. No four o'clock frown or anything, or at least I didn't notice it, because I got busy with my chores the minute I walked in the door. I even thought I heard Momma whistle half a song, and she sure wouldn't be whistling if Mrs. Pie had called. I was so scared that the phone would ring at dinner, I couldn't even eat my dessert. It was pie, wouldn't you know, a "celebrating-the-first-week-of-school" sour cherry pie. Sour is what it was, all right. How did Momma always seem to know exactly what was going on?

Every time I tried to take a bite of the pie, I felt prickles again in my throat.

I did my homework after dinner, took my bath, and even flossed my teeth to save Momma money at the dentist. God likes it when you do things like saving your momma money. When he counts up your good and bad deeds at the end of the day, it can't hurt to have some extra good.

Following that same thinking, I went to sleep early, too. Momma asked if I felt sick. Eight o'clock on a Friday night? "Maybe I have a tapeworm," I said. I told Momma how Shorn L.'s brother got a tapeworm from taking a bite out of the belly of a live fish he hooked in the river. "Shorn L. says tapeworms make you want to fall asleep all the time."

"You have a tapeworm like I have a million dollars," she said, and closed my shades, and tucked me into bed.

But I couldn't sleep. The cicadas sounded like whispering behind my back. The cars sounded like Shorn L.'s scolding. Shorn L. said she would tell on Rolly and also Patty if I didn't. I had no idea that Patty had a hand in the cheating, but Shorn L. told me that she saw Patty and Rolly toss notes back and forth at least three times, and Hugo saw it at least once. I begged Shorn L. not to tell anyone anything. I said, "Think of it like I was giving Rolly some charity." Shorn L. snorted in my face and called me a crazy fool.

The day played over and over in my mind like a bad movie. I couldn't sleep. And then I heard it: *plip*. A small dripping sound. Or dropping sound. I knew right away what it was even though I'd never heard it before. I got up and looked in my closet. One of my stars had fallen down. I picked it up and pulled my desk chair over to the closet.

I took my stars down.

Mrs. Young?

This is Kath Maloo. Hate to bother you at home, but some moms are worried. Cheating, in Mrs. Pie's class. Jenna Lee cheated on the district math test, but it seems Mrs. Pie didn't do anything about it.

People say Shorn L. was also involved. Some moms have called me, since I'm PTA president—

What a terrible shame! I cannot believe that Mrs. Pie didn't even tell me herself, but she is, well—

Yes, Mrs. Young, I know what you mean, but don't you think that Mrs. Pie should've done something about it? Set an example?

Absolutely, Kath. Thank you, Kath, for letting me know about this. I'm going to take care of it right away!

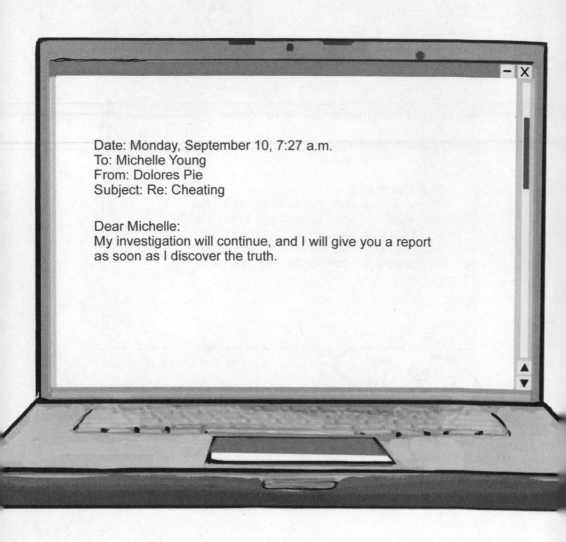

Date: Monday, September 10, 7:27 a.m.
To: Michelle Young
From: Dolores Pie
Subject: Re: Cheating

Dear Michelle:
My investigation will continue, and I will give you a report
as soon as I discover the truth.

7 The Bad News

On Monday Rolly was pinker than ever, which was perfect since Rolly Maloo and Patty got the two top math scores. Mrs. Pie said she was proud of how the class did as a whole, especially on some of the questions that seemed near impossible. "I had a hard time figuring out number eight," she said, "but three of you were able to get the right answer!

"Unfortunately," she said, "there will not be any district math competition this year." That made me very sad, until I realized I probably would not get to go anyway, because of the cheating. Patty looked as mad as an old horse getting new shoes nailed on. I guess she was counting on it. Rolly's mouth dropped open and some drool dribbled on her lace.

Then the really bad news came. During recess, Mrs. Pie kept Hugo, Shorn L., and me inside for a meeting. I wondered if this was going to be a "cheating meeting." But it was worse than that.

Mrs. Pie told us that the district was starting an experimental new math program for kids who did not pass the test. I almost passed the test. I got every answer right up to and including number eight, but I got every answer wrong after that. I did not like the sound of "experimental." It made me feel like a rat. The three of us did not pass the test, so at least we would be rats in the same cage.

We would be doing an extra hour of math each day. Ordinarily I would love to do an extra hour of math each day, but not if we would have to skip our hour of specials. No art? No music? No PE? No basketball? No soccer? No track? No PE was going to just kill me. Momma would never let me do sports after school, with all my chores and the cost of being on a team. No art would kill Hugo. Hugo's family could never afford the paints and fancy brushes and canvas board that we used in art. Shorn L. didn't care much for art or music or PE, but two hours of math a day would kill Shorn L., for sure.

Four things that could ruin my life:

1. No PE
2. Hugo and Shorn L. killed by extra math
3. Momma figuring out what I did
4. Mrs. Pie not liking me anymore

"I'm going to do my best to change this new program," Mrs. Pie said. "I don't want my students to miss PE and art and music. For now, though, this is what we're going to do: I worked all morning to get special permission from the district so you three can take the test again on Friday. For the next four days, I want you coming here an hour early and staying an hour late. I'll bring doughnuts and juice in the morning and cookies and milk for after school. I'll call your parents and tell them it's a special math project. Jenna, you'll be the teacher. Hugo and Shorn L., you let Jenna explain percents and fractions and decimals to you. She knows them better than I do! You're going to pass that test, all three of you—but no passing notes this time!"

I must have looked in an awful state of shock because Mrs. Pie told me to go outside and get myself a drink of water and rest in the shade. She asked Shorn L. and Hugo to stay another minute. When I walked outside, I realized that I had not been in a state of shock yet because now, all of sudden, I could feel true shock setting in. Momma was there, with Shorn L.'s momma, walking side by side with Mrs. Young. And they were not smiling.

Let's just say I saw notes being passed around by two girls who were not Jenna.

So I hope you test everybody for their number nine, including Rolly and Patty, and see if anybody looks like they're disguising their writing.

Have you been watching too many TV crime shows, Detective Loop? Why would Rolly and Patty be interested in cheating?

To get the high scores. To go to the math contest.

But this year there is no contest.

We didn't know that until this morning. Mrs. Pie, maybe you might want to ask if they can explain how they got their number eight answers, with that question being so impossible and all.

Shorn L., do me a favor. Tell Rolly and Patty to come here immediately!

Right away, Mrs. Pie!

8 Detective Loop

Shorn L. came out of Mrs. Pie's room with a smile in her eyes, but her smile disappeared in a hurry when she saw the mommas and Mrs. Young coming our way. "I'm going to bring Rolly and Patty," she said. "Mrs. Pie wants to question them." Shorn L. ran fast, which was quite a sight, since the only thing Shorn L. does fast is eat her cookies and cake.

Momma came at me with a twisted face. I could tell she'd been arguing with Mrs. Young. Mrs. Loop looked disgusted, like someone who had eaten too much grease for breakfast. Mrs. Young had a smile on, a laughing-at-you smile just like the office lady gives. She was staring at something behind me. Someone. I turned around, just as Mrs. Pie put her hand on my shoulder.

77

"Go play, Jenna," Mrs. Pie said. "You too, Hugo. You still have ten minutes of recess. Don't worry about your mother. I didn't call her, or Mrs. Loop, but now that they've been called, I'll set things straight."

I made my biggest "sorry" face at Momma. I knew she was probably mad from shame more than anything else, and I kicked myself (yes, actually kicked myself, even if accidentally) for not telling her what had happened. When I was little, Momma always used to tell me that the only thing worse than doing something dumb is doing something dumb and being too much of a coward to admit it.

She stopped saying it because I stopped doing dumb things. Either that or I got better at admitting I'd done them. I wish I could go back to being five years old again, when the dumbest thing I did was break a vase or lose a library book. I wish I could go back to Friday. When I got the "What's #8?" note, I would tear it up in fifty little pieces and throw it down on the floor. I would curse Rolly Maloo for using me to cheat and never want to be her friend.

Shorn L. came back with Rolly and Patty, but Mrs. Pie was busy talking with the mommas and Mrs. Young. Shorn L. didn't care. She opened the door and ordered Rolly and Patty to go in. She made me go, too, marching in after us like a prison guard. Mrs. Young stopped talking and looked at us like we had no business being there. But Shorn L. had courage. "Mrs. Pie, Mrs. Young, Mrs. Lee, and Momma," she said, "I brought Rolly and Patty here to do their number nines for you."

"Thank you, Shorn L.," Mrs. Pie said. "If you two girls could just write number nine here for me, please."

"What does this have to do with anything?" Mrs. Young asked, growing more frustrated by the minute. Mrs. Young is the kind of person who likes to be in charge of things, but Mrs. Pie wasn't letting her take control.

"You told me to do an investigation, and I'm doing it, Mrs. Young. I'd like these girls to write the number mark, and then the number nine," Mrs. Pie said, "and then I'd like them to show us how they solved the answer to question number eight on the test, too."

By now recess was over, and the whole class had gathered outside the windows, pressing their noses and ears against the glass. Mrs. Parker and Mrs. Maloo were scurrying across the courtyard, heading from the PTA office toward our room. They barged into the room, babbling, but Mrs. Pie shushed them up.

Rolly wrote the number mark and then the number nine, but not anything like normal. She wrote it all slanted and curlicued. It didn't look like her writing. Patty wrote it normal.

"Just write in your normal writing, Rolly," Mrs. Pie said.

"Write in your normal writing, honey," Mrs. Maloo said.

"That is my normal writing," Rolly said in a voice that sounded like it was asking a question.

Mrs. Pie took a pile of homework out of her desk. "Strange," Mrs. Pie said. "On your homework, your number nine looks quite different. You wouldn't be trying to disguise your writing, would you?"

"Why would she do that?" Mrs. Maloo said. "Mrs. Pie, this is outrageous!"

"It just seems odd, Mrs. Maloo, that Rolly's number nine on her weekend homework looks very much like the number nine on this note, a note that was thrown at Jenna Lee during the test. And yet Rolly's number nine today doesn't look like any single number nine she wrote all last week."

"That proves nothing," Mrs. Maloo said.

Suddenly Mrs. Pie noticed the other kids looking inside the room, pressing their hands and faces against the windows. "Excuse me," she said. "Let me take the other children to the library for a few minutes. I'll be right back."

It was quiet when Mrs. Pie was gone, nobody talking. She was just gone for a minute, maybe less, but it seemed like one hour. Nervous time stretches long, just like a rubber band.

When Mrs. Pie returned, she got down to business fast. "Let's move on, then. Rolly and Patty, can you show us how you got the answer to question number eight? Only three students in the whole class got that answer right, as you know: you two and Jenna Lee. Rolly, take the left side of the board. Patty, take the right side of the board. Here's the problem. Show us your work, please."

Rolly and Patty struggled for five minutes that seemed like fifteen and got nowhere. It was painful to watch them squirm and itch with us watching, but boy, did I love it. I didn't realize I could be so mean. Maybe it's not being mean, though, when justice is involved. Gosh, Mrs. Pie was like a regular Crime Scene Queen.

"Jenna, please go up to the board and show how it's done," Mrs. Pie said. I did. When I turned to see Momma's face, I expected to see a smile. Or tears. Instead I saw her angry face again, angrier than ever!

I put the marker down, and Mrs. Pie asked me to tell everyone what happened. I knew I should tell, but I didn't want Momma to hear it in front of everybody. Besides, the story was so long and complicated, and it would've sounded so dumb to say, "She looked so sick and forlorn." So I said nothing. I just looked down at my shoes.

"Shorn L., will you tell us what you saw?" Mrs. Pie said.

I held my breath. "Don't tell, Shorn L., please don't!" I said before I could stop the words from coming out.

Shorn L. didn't even look my way. "Hugo was making sick sounds, Mrs. Pie, so I turned around. Turned and saw Patty pass a note—"

"That is a lie!" Patty shrieked.

"Let my daughter finish!" Mrs. Loop said.

"Please go on, Shorn L.," Mrs. Pie said. "What else?"

"Patty passed a note to Rolly. Rolly passed a

note back to Patty, and Patty to Rolly, and then Rolly threw a note to Jenna. Jenna paused a really long time. I knew she was all torn up and didn't want to give Rolly an answer, but Rolly made a face at her. Jenna wrote an answer down and threw it to Rolly. Rolly gave the answer to Patty, then Rolly threw another note at Jenna. That's when Jenna stood up, and you caught her."

"One big lie," Patty said. "Lies, lies, lies." Rolly said nothing.

"I think we should continue this discussion privately," Mrs. Young said.

Shorn L.'s mother said, "I think the truth is coming out fine right here."

"It was Patty's idea!" Rolly said.

"Rolly!" Patty screamed. "You liar!"

"It *was* all your idea, Patty! How can you call me a liar?" Poor Rolly, she had started sobbing and could hardly breathe. Her mother looked like a wolverine. Patty's mother looked like a wolverine, too. Patty looked like a baby wolverine, and Rolly looked like a mouse in a trap. I was back to feeling sorry for her again. Correction: Rat in a trap, I said to myself. Rat!

Mrs. Young shrunk up, all wrinkled like a day-old balloon. She told the Wolverine Mommas and the Good Mommas that it was time to leave. The Wolverine Mommas were fighting mad and ready to take a bite out of someone, but Mrs. Young patted their arms and calmed them down. Mrs. Pie thanked the Good Mommas for coming, and told all the mommas that she'd call them at lunchtime to finish the discussion.

Momma's face was softer now. She even came up to me and gave my hand a little squeeze before leaving.

9 Me and Shorn L.

In the lunch line, Rolly shot me a look so guilty and sorry it made her hair shake. It almost looked like a smile, impossible as that may seem. The funny thing is, I did not smile back. She could have asked me to her house right then, and I would have said no thank you.

Shorn L. sat down with her spaghetti and chocolate cake and two milks. Last year the cafeteria lady started giving Shorn L. an extra milk on account of Shorn L. is so short, but so far it doesn't seem to be helping any, especially since she usually trades her milk for anybody's cookie or cake. "Why did Mrs. Pie make you stay behind just now?"

"She thanked me for coming out with the

truth," Shorn L. said. "She could tell I was having a hard time with being a fink.

"Mrs. Pie told me I should start writing detective stories. And she also said that Hugo and I need to pass that test. So you better teach us right, Jenna Lee. No joke."

Shorn L. ate her cake first, before her spaghetti, and then drank down her milk. All done in less than a minute flat, including the burp. After she finished her first milk, she traded her second milk to Hugo for his chocolate cake.

"Now you're happy I told the truth, isn't that right? Am I a good friend, or am I a good friend?" Shorn L. said. I did not say a thing, but sometimes there isn't any need.

I gave Shorn L. half my apple, and she gave me Hugo's cake—minus a little corner, just about 10 percent.

10 Momma's Pies

Momma sent word for Mrs. Pie to have me and Shorn L. walk home to my house together after our after-school math. This struck me as mighty strange since I never have anyone over to the house. When we got home, though, I saw that this was not strange at all compared to the even stranger sight before our eyes. "Why don't you two grab a soda pop and play a while," Momma said. "I'll be done with these last two pies in twenty minutes."

Momma was baking pies. Pies, pies, pies! There were pies on the table, on the counter, on the TV, on the chairs—pies sitting everywhere where Momma's work envelopes usually are. What's going on? I wondered, but I didn't want to ask questions because I didn't want to answer any, either. It was strange, though: your momma finds out that you cheated at school, and hid the fact of being caught, and instead of punishing you first thing, she has you bring a friend over for soda pop and greets you with her hands full of pies.

"Go get your wagon from the storage shed and clean it up," she said to me. "We've got some pies to deliver. But tell me first which kind you want. There are eight kinds: chocolate cream, banana cream, sour cherry, cinnamon apple, sweet potato, pecan, lemon meringue, and peach—one of each. Shorn L., one of these is a thank-you pie for you, for speaking up. Please choose your favorite." Shorn L. picked the cinnamon apple. I picked the pecan on account of it being such a nutty day. Besides, pecan is one of Momma's favorites, though she would never save one for herself.

"Let's take these to your house, Shorn L., for your momma's restaurant," Momma said.

"I'll just call Momma and have her pick them up in her car."

"I don't want to trouble her. She's done too much as it is."

"Momma won't mind. And if she picks up the

pies in the car, she can deliver them straight-away to the Over-There."

Shorn L.'s momma was at our house in five minutes. We loaded up the back of her station wagon with pies, using scrunched-up paper towels to keep the pies from sliding into each other. Shorn L. sat with her own cinnamon apple thank-you pie in the front seat. It looked like the pie might not make it home.

Momma flopped down at the kitchen table like a tired old baker's apron, with smudges of chocolate and cherry and sweet potato on her face and arms, and flour in her hair. "You sit, too," she said. "Time to talk."

We talked for almost an hour that stretched out like one of those super-deluxe rubber bands they use to move refrigerators.

Things I was smart enough to say:
1. Sorry
2. I was wrong
3. Hugo and Shorn L. are finally learning percents, thanks to me
4. I like being a teacher!

Things I maybe shouldn't have said:
1. But Rolly looked so forlorn
2. And now nobody's talking to her or Patty
3. And I feel bad

"That's good," Momma said. "Now talk about what I want to hear."

So I talked about the math test. I told her how hard it was for me to decide what to do. I told her about charity. She snorted, too, just like Shorn L.

"Did Rolly apologize to you?" Momma asked.

"No," I said. I felt ashamed to say so.

"I'm going to call Rolly's mother and demand

an apology. Make her say she's sorry for the trouble she caused you. I'm going to call her up right now." Momma grabbed the phone.

"No, Momma, please don't. It was my fault, too, for giving her the answer. I just wanted a friend." Momma let it drop. I made us ham sandwiches for dinner, and took my shower, and did my homework, and gave her a hug before going to bed.

"Awfully early for bed," she said. "Tapeworm?"

I said, "Momma, did you win a million dollars?"

11 The Math Test, Round Two

Shorn L. and Hugo were like horses in the gate at the Kentucky Derby, all wound up with jitters. I could understand why Shorn L. didn't want to be quizzed, but I was proud of Hugo for trying. Seemed to me that they both could use every extra second of practice right up until the start of the test.

I finished today's math test in fifteen minutes. I didn't turn it in early, though, because I didn't want to make Shorn L. and Hugo nervous, wondering how I could possibly be done so fast when they were probably still on question number five or six. So I went back and checked my work over once, then twice.

There were still ten minutes left, so I settled

into some daydreaming. I thought about how much I enjoyed walking to school by myself each morning. (Now that I had to be there extra early, way too early for sleepyhead Momma, she finally agreed to let me walk on my own.) I thought about how much I enjoyed teaching Shorn L. and Hugo. I thought about how much they'd learned in just four days. I thought about what Mrs. Pie said, that she knew two families who might pay me to tutor their second and third graders after school in math, and a third family who might not be able to pay but would let me ride their horse, if I was interested. If I was interested! Is pie sweet?

I looked over at Hugo. He wasn't sick at all this morning, I swear it, but now he looked like he was suffering shivers and sweats. I glanced over at Shorn L. She was chewing on her pencil.

Mrs. Pie gave us a one-minute warning. Hugo and Shorn L. were bubbling in their Number 2 pencil marks fast. I decided to pray:

Dear God, I am sorry for the cheating,
but I think you've forgiven me because so much
goodness is coming of it, like the teaching you let me do,
and the tutoring for horse riding, and Momma's pies.

If Momma and Mrs. Loop had never been
called into the principal's office, they never would've
talked about pies, and Momma would still be stuffing
envelopes every night instead of filling our house with
the heavenly smell of chocolate and cherry and
banana and pumpkin and lime.

And now Shorn L. gets to come over once a week,
and I get to go to her house, and her brothers
don't even bother me with ground-up bugs.

Of course you know the real reason for this prayer,
don't you? Please let Shorn L. and Hugo pass,
oh, please do. Amen.

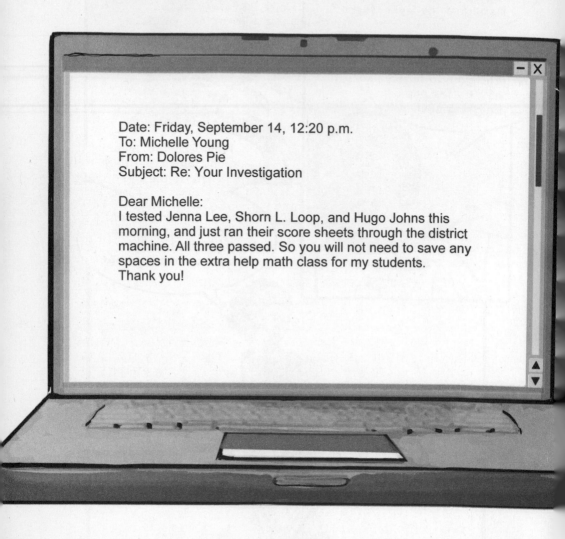

Date: Friday, September 14, 12:20 p.m.
To: Michelle Young
From: Dolores Pie
Subject: Re: Your Investigation

Dear Michelle:
I tested Jenna Lee, Shorn L. Loop, and Hugo Johns this morning, and just ran their score sheets through the district machine. All three passed. So you will not need to save any spaces in the extra help math class for my students.
Thank you!

12 The Results

Turns out Shorn L. and Hugo passed the math test. I did, too, with 100 percent. Mrs. Pie came at the tail end of lunch to give us the good news. She sat down, swung her legs round, and put a chocolate cream pie on the table with plastic spoons. "Your mother brought me two pies just now," she said. "She said they could be for the bake sale, but she'd rather that I took them as her thank-you gift. We put one on the bake sale table, but I think we should eat this one right now, don't you?"

Hugo let out a big "Hoo-YA!" He grabbed a spoon and shoveled a mountain out of the pie. Shorn L. grabbed a spoon and took out a piece that was as tall as it was wide. I didn't think it would fit in her mouth, but I had no idea how big a mouth she has. After that, it was all big mouths and laughing voices and hands reaching and arms around me, grabbing spoonfuls of sweet, sweet thank you.

JANET S. WONG is the acclaimed author of dozens of books for young readers, including *Dumpster Diver, Apple Pie 4th of July,* and the Minn & Jake series. She lives near Princeton, New Jersey, with her husband and son. Visit her at **www.janetwong.com**.

ELIZABETH BUTTLER is a freelance illustrator, character and set designer, and fabricator for stop-motion animation. She lives with her husband and son in the Berkshire Hills in western Massachusetts. Visit her at **www.elizabethbuttler.com**.